PEANUTS
Best of Friends
By Charles M. Schulz

Charlie Brown had a great big smile on his face. It was the weekend, and he couldn't wait to spend it with his buddies.

HAPPINESS IS HAVING FUN WITH YOUR FRIENDS!

He picked up his baseball glove and went to see if Linus wanted to play catch.

But Linus had promised to help
Sally with her homework . . .

"*Never mind,*" **said Charlie Brown.**
"*I'll go and see if Lucy wants to play.*"

Lucy was with Schroeder, chatting away.
"Hi, Lucy," said Charlie Brown. "Do you want to go to the park?"
"Sorry, Charlie Brown," she replied.
"I'm busy listening to Schroeder!"

"This is what you call listening?" sighed Schroeder.

"Maybe Peppermint Patty will want to play," thought Charlie Brown.

Charlie Brown found Peppermint Patty,
but Marcie was helping her study for a test . . .

On his way home, Charlie Brown found Rerun throwing a ball against a wall. "*Do you want to play a game?*" asked Charlie Brown.

"*I'm practising my wall-bouncing skills,*" said Rerun. "*I'll buy you an ice cream,*" offered Charlie Brown. "*Sorry, Charlie Brown,*" replied Rerun. "*I'm too busy.*"

"How can anyone be too busy for ice cream?" **sighed Charlie Brown.** *"Good grief!"*

NOBODY LIKES ME.

Charlie Brown felt lonely. All his friends were busy rushing here and there, and no one had time to play with him.

"I guess I'll just go and sit at
home on my own," he sighed.

Charlie Brown sat glumly on the sofa and tried sharing his feelings . . .

But the plant wasn't really listening.

RING!

Just as Charlie Brown
switched on the TV,
the phone rang.

WOOF!
THANKS, SNOOPY. I NEEDED TO HEAR A FRIENDLY VOICE... YES, OF COURSE I HAVE COOKIES...

Snoopy and Charlie Brown settled down to watch a movie together with a giant box of cookies.

THE FRIENDSHIP OF A BOY AND HIS DOG IS A BEAUTIFUL THING.

Just then, the door opened and there were all of Charlie Brown's friends. "*Turns out we weren't that busy after all,*" said Lucy. "*Let's play!*"

"Err, come in, everybody," **began Charlie Brown.** *"Great to see you, but we were just going to watch some TV."*

"Ooh, cookies!" **said Lucy.**

Soon the sofa was packed, with everyone jostling and chatting away noisily.

"It's great hanging out with good friends . . ."
Charlie Brown said to Snoopy.

". . . but nothing beats hanging out with your best friend!"
IT JUST DOESN'T GET ANY BETTER THAN THIS.